# CARNY GAMES 1

---

A SEX PARTY

JADE'S EROTIC ADVENTURES
BOOK 49

VICTORIA RUSH

# VOLUME 49

JADE'S EROTIC ADVENTURES - BOOK 49

# COPYRIGHT

# ALSO BY VICTORIA RUSH

**Adult Fairytales:**

The Enchanted Forest: An Erotic Fairytale

The Land of Giants: An Erotic Fairytale

The Dragon's Lair: An Erotic Fairytale

Witch's Brew: An Erotic Fairytale

The Mage's Spell: An Erotic Fairytale

The Mermaid Lagoon: An Erotic Fairytale

The Coven: An Erotic Fairytale

Rapunzel: An Erotic Fairytale

The Seven Dwarfs: An Erotic Fairytale

The Land of Mutants: An Erotic Fairytale

The Erotic Temple: A Sexy Fairytale (Coming Soon)

**Erotica Themed Bundles:**

Voyeur: Lesbian Erotica Bundle

Public Affairs: A Lesbian Anthology

Futa Fantasies: The Ladyboy Collection

Threesomes: The Lesbian Collection

Threesomes - Volume 2: The Lesbian Collection

First Time: A Lesbian Anthology

Hedonism: An Erotic Anthology

Switch Hitters: Bisexual Erotica

Taboo Erotica: The Lesbian Series

BDSM: The Lesbian Collection

Party Games: The Erotic Collection

Party Games 2: The Erotic Collection

All Girl 1: Lesbian Erotica Bundle

All Girl 2: Lesbian Erotica Bundle

All Girl 3: Lesbian Erotica Bundle

All Girl 4: Lesbian Erotica Bundle

**Erotic Fairytale Bundles:**

Clover's Fantasy Adventures: Books 1 - 5

Clover's Fantasy Adventures: Books 6 - 10

**Erotic Fantasy:**

Pirate's Bounty: A Time Travel Adventure

Wild West: A Time Travel Adventure

Private Riley: A Time Travel Adventure

Cleopatra's Secret: A Time Travel Adventure

Bounty Hunter 2125: A Time Travel Adventure

Ninja Assassin: A Time Travel Adventure

The 300: A Time Travel Adventure

Arabian Nights: An Erotic Fairytale (coming soon...)

**Steamy Time Travel Bundles:**

Riley's Time Travel Adventures: Books 1 - 5

Lesbian Erotica:

The Dinner Party: Lesbian Voyeur Erotica

The Darkroom: Bisexual Voyeur Erotica

Naked Yoga: Lesbian Transgender Erotica

Nude Cruise: Bisexual Voyeur Erotica

Rush Hour: Taboo Public Sex

The Girl Next Door: First Time Lesbian Erotic Romance

Girls' Camp: Lesbian Group Sex

Wet Dream: Ladyboy Fantasy Erotica

The Convent: Taboo Sex with a Nun

Sex Robot: A Dream Sex Machine

The Personal Trainer: Getting Pumped at the Gym

The Dominatrix: BDSM Lesbian Domination

Webcam Chat: Lesbian Online Sex

Paint Me: A Kinky Bodypainting Workshop

The Toy Party: Girls Sharing Sex Toys

The Costume Party: Strapping One On

Swedish Sauna: Lesbian Group Sex

The Therapist: Taboo Lesbian Erotica

Elevator Shaft: Bisexual Threesomes Erotica

Ladyboy: Lesbian Transgender Erotica

Peep Show: Lesbian Voyeur Erotica

The Dare: Public Sex Erotica

Maid Service: Lesbian Threesomes Erotica

The Hitchhiker: First Time Lesbian Erotica

The Housesitter: Spycam Lesbian Erotica

The Spa: Lesbian Group Orgy

Parlor Games: Blindfold Sex Party

The Exchange Student: First Time Lesbian Erotica

The Hostel: Bisexual Group Erotica

The Harem: Lesbian Erotic Romance

The Orient Express: Lesbian Voyeur Erotica

The First Lady: A Forbidden Lesbian Erotic Romance

The Slave: Lesbian BDSM Erotica

The Masseuse: Lesbian Sensuous Erotica

Too Close for Comfort: Lesbian Forbidden Erotica

Naked Twister: A Wild Party Game

Lexi: The Sex App ( Lesbian Fantasy Erotica )

Call Girl: Lesbian Bisexual Threesomes Erotica

Circle Jill: Lesbian Masturbation Workshop

The Viewing Room: Masturbation Voyeur Erotica

Spin the Bottle: A Kinky Party Game

The Hair Salon: Lesbian Voyeur Erotica

Tribadism 1: Girls Only Sex Workshop

Tribadism 2: The Art of Scissoring

Tribadism 3: Threeway Hookups

The Kiss: A Game of Oral Sex

Pledge Week: Sorority Sisters

Carny Games 1: A Wild Sex Party

Carny Games 2: A Kinky Sex Party

Carny Games 3: An Erotic Sex Party

Dreamscape: An Artificial Reality Game

Glory Hole: Guess Who's On the Other Side

Joy Ride: A Late Night Erotic Bus Trip

The Blind Girl: An Erotic Romance(Coming Soon)

**Lesbian Erotica Bundles:**

Jade's Erotic Adventures: Books 1 - 5

Jade's Erotic Adventures: Books 6 - 10

Jade's Erotic Adventures: Books 11 - 15

Jade's Erotic Adventures: Books 16 - 20

Jade's Erotic Adventures: Books 21 - 25

Jade's Erotic Adventures: Books 26 - 30

Jade's Erotic Adventures: Books 31 - 35

Jade's Erotic Adventures: Books 36 - 40

Jade's Erotic Adventures: Books 41 - 45

Jade's Erotic Adventures: Books 46 - 50

Fifty Shades of Jade: Superbundle

**Standalone Stories:**

The Polynesian Girl: A Lesbian EroticRomance

*For the uninhibited...*

# WANT TO AMP UP YOUR SEX LIFE?

*Sign up for my newsletter to receive more free books and other steamy stuff. Discover a hundred different ways to wet your whistle!*

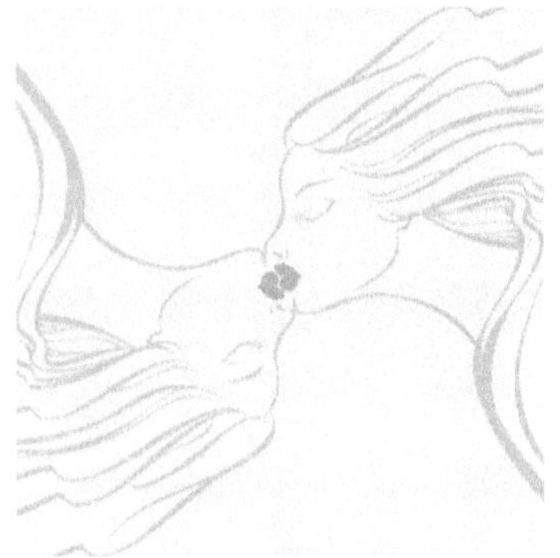

Victoria Rush Erotica

**1**

———

When I received a new invitation from my friend Madison, I couldn't wait to open the message. She always hosted the sexiest parties, and with the cryptic heading Carny Games, I could already feel my panties moistening as I began to read the message.

*Dear Jade,*

*You are cordially invited to a party at my place this Saturday evening starting at 9 p.m.*

*The theme of this event is Carnival Games, where everyone will participate in erotic contests simulating county fair games.*

*From Ring Toss to Ping Pong Basketball, Whack-a-Mole, Hands-free Jenga, Bobbing for Peaches, and many more, these games will make you laugh and squeal in equal measure.*

*But these contests aren't for the faint of heart, so be prepared to take your clothes off and let it all hang out. And remember to park your inhibitions at the door, because there's no telling who you'll be paired up with. From boy-on-girl to girl-on-girl to boy-on-boy to other surprise pairings, you can be sure to stretch your imagination in more ways than one.*

*So come clean, come prepared, and come often. Because we're going to have a ribald and riotous good time!*

*RSVP before Thursday,*

*Maddy*

*P.S.: Please bring a personal dick pic or pussy pic (twenty copies each), fully erect and shaved if possible. This will be used for a special game of the Pin the Tail on the Donkey.*


Holy fuck! I thought after reading her message. What has she dreamed up this time? Ping Pong Basketball? Bobbing for Peaches?

I could guess what might be involved in the Ring Toss game and Whack-a-Mole, but the other ones sounded vaguely female-centric. Of course, Hands-free Jenga didn't leave much to the imagination. The idea of watching a bunch of guys competing to see how long they could keep a tower of bricks from falling over by poking out the blocks one at a time with their hard dicks sounded erotic and hilarious at the same time.

But the Pin the Tail on the Donkey game had me stumped. What was she going to do with the dick and pussy pictures? And what were these 'other pairings' she alluded to in her message? Was it possible that one or more of my favorite t-girls would also be invited to the party? The combinations seemed almost endless.

As my mind began to wander about what she had planned, my hand slipped under my panties, imagining who I'd be paired up with doing what kind of depraved activities in front of the entire group.

Bring it on, Maddy, I thought, curling my fingers into my hole. I'll be coming, alright. Sooner than you expect...

WHEN I ARRIVED at Madison's house on the night of the party, she collected my pics then escorted me to the living room where a group of twenty people lounged around, sipping wine. I recognized some of the faces in the crowd, but there were quite a few new people I hadn't seen before. With an even sprinkling of men and women, I scanned the crowd while everybody made small talk introducing themselves.

In addition to my friends Lily, Bonnie, and Emma, there was the sexy neighbor couple from the last party, Brad and Laura, plus my old friends from work, Ryan, Neil, and Marco. But it was the new faces in the crowd that attracted most of my attention. With a mix of black, white, Asian, and Hispanic hotties, my pussy was already throbbing in antici-pation of the coming pairings. Rounding out the group was my transgender friend Shae and the full-figured Christina Hendricks lookalike from my tribbing workshop, Paige.

As my eyes darted around the room, I suddenly became conscious of the growing wet spot in the crotch of my jeans. Sitting down on the sofa to take the last available spot, I nudged next to Shae, crossing my legs in embarrassment.

"I see you've already started planning your hookups," she smiled, glancing down at the stain in my crotch.

"I could fuck just about any one of these knockouts," I nodded, taking the large glass of chardonnay she handed me. "Although something tells me the decision is going to be out of my hands for most of the night."

AFTER THE LAST GUEST ARRIVED, Madison carried the stack of photos into the kitchen, making short notations on the back of each one, then she carried the pile into the living room, distributing one dick pic to each woman and one pussy pick to each man. Shae peered at her picture, noticing a man's erect cock, and smiled.

"I guess I'll be playing the girl part for this game," she said.

"Lucky you," I nodded, glancing at the picture of a large, caramel-colored hard-on flapping up against the rippled abs of some unidentified stud whose face had been cut out of the picture. "You'll have dealer's choice for the rest of the night."

I peered at my photo showing a huge, dark-colored erection, then turned the picture over. Notated on the back next to a loop of sticky tape was the single letter 'H'.

"Any idea what the letters mean?" Shae said, pinching her eyebrows at the inscription on the back of her photo.

"No idea," I said, noticing Madison taking a seat at the head of the group. "But I have a feeling we're about to find out."

"Good evening, everybody," Madison smiled, peering around the room at the group squinting at their cards with an equal mix of curiosity and distraction. "Thank you all for coming and for bringing your intimate photos. First of all, let me assure you that these pictures will never leave this room and that they'll be safely disposed of after everyone leaves the party."

"Whew," Marco sighed. "I was having nightmares of my dick pic circulating on the internet while everyone speculated about who it belonged to."

The group chuckled, and Madison nodded with a knowing grin.

"Well, you're at least half right about your concerns," she said. "But we'll get to that part in a moment. First, let's take a few minutes to introduce ourselves, since not everyone knows each other. Tell us your name, where you're from, and what's your connection to the group. And to make it more interesting, I'd like every person to tell one truth and one lie about themselves. Later on, we'll try to guess which is which. Who'd like to go first?"

Never one to be shy, Shae raised her hand and Madison nodded in her direction.

"Hello," Shae said. "My name is Shae, and I'm originally from Missouri. I was introduced to members of this group by my good friend, Jade. Something you may not know about me is that I have an extra Y chromosome, which means I have both male and female reproductive organs. But even though I'm equipped to have sex with both genders, I've only ever been intimate with men."

"Hmm," Madison said after Shae finished introducing herself. "That's an interesting puzzle. We'll have to see which one of those statements is a lie and which one is the truth before the evening is over. Who'd like to go next?"

As each member of the group proceeded to introduce themselves, everyone listened to their brief profiles, chuckling softly at their self-effacing disclosures. By the time we finished with the handsome married couple Brad and Laura, we had a pretty good idea which of their joint declarations about each being their first and only sexual partner was a truth versus a lie.

"Alright then," Maddy said after everybody finished. "Now that we've scratched the surface of everyone's identity, let's see if we can begin to peel back some of the layers. I'm sure you're all eager to learn what we're going to do with the intimate pictures you've taken of yourselves. In our first game I like to call Shower versus Grower, we're going to ask the men to strip down naked and line up against the wall while the women examine their dick pics and try to match the erect penises with their flaccid ones."

Madison paused as she peered around the group, surveying the surprised expressions on the faces of the men.

"Who's ready to get this party started?"

**2**

———

"I assume because you've given me a dick pic instead of a pussy pic that you'd like me to be on the other side of the lineup for this game?" Shae said.

"With your unique sexual anatomy, it would be a little too easy to guess your identity," Madison nodded. "But don't worry, we'll get you involved in the other side of the action soon enough."

"And you expect us to remain soft the whole time these women are inspecting our dicks?" Brad said.

"That's half the fun," Maddy smiled. "There's a reason why we're naming this contest Shower versus Grower. We wouldn't want to spoil the mystery too fast."

Ryan grunted as he squirmed in his chair, adjusting his package uncomfortably.

"It might be kind of hard..." he said, clearing his throat at the obvious pun. "To keep from getting turned on while all these beautiful women are staring at our dicks," he said.

"I guess that's where we'll separate the men from the boys," Maddy said, glancing at his bulging crotch. "If you get too aroused during the inspection, you'll be automatically disqualified."

"Will there be a prize for the winner?" Marco asked. "At the county fair, we usually get a stuffed toy for winning each of the contests."

"Oh, there'll be a prize, alright," Madison grinned. "And it will be plenty soft and squishy. But this one will be infinitely more fun to nuzzle up next to."

I glanced at my photo and peered around the room, already beginning to narrow the list of likely matches.

"So, once we think we've identified the correct matching penis, how do we go about indicating our choice?" I said.

"Simply stick the back of your photo somewhere on your target's body," Maddy nodded. "Then I'll compare the identification symbols on the reverse side to see who guessed it right."

"Will this be a timed contest?" Bonnie said.

"I think it will have to be," Madison said. "With so many delicious penises on display, you ladies won't ever want to stop inspecting the goods. Plus, the longer it goes, the harder it'll be for the men to keep themselves composed."

"That's one way of putting it," Neil said as everybody in the room chuckled.

"Okay then," Madison said, turning on the living room TV and pairing her phone's electronic timer to the display. "You'll have exactly five minutes to match the flaccid penis with the erect one. Are you guys ready?"

"What if we're already half-erect?" Ryan said.

"Then you better start thinking about dead cats or your naked grandmother," Maddy laughed. "Because if you want to have a chance at putting that thing to better use, you'll have to maintain your composure a little longer."

Then she pointed to the opposite wall and nodded.

"Alright, you guys know the rules. Strip down naked and line up shoulder to shoulder on the far wall. When everybody has their clothes off, I'll start the timer."

The men peered at one another for a moment, then they slowly began to strip down, positioning themselves against the wall like a bunch of perps in a police lineup.

"Okay, ladies," Madison smiled, nodding at the row of naked studs standing awkwardly next to one another. "Have at it."

The women raised up out of their seats then queued up in single file to the left of the lineup, glancing at their photos and the flaccid penises of each of the candidates as they moved slowly down the line. Some of the men closed their eyes and scrunched up their faces, trying to distract themselves from the sight of ten beautiful women parading in front of their naked bodies, but for the most part they managed to keep themselves composed while their counterparts teased and cajoled them.

"Are you sure that thing is fully soft?" Shae teased Ryan, who was standing stiff as a brick with his hands resting tightly by his side like he was participating in a military inspection. "Because it already looks as big as some of the hard-ons I've seen."

"I guess that means I'm a shower," Ryan shrugged.

"That's too bad," Shae grinned. "I was kind of hoping to see it in its full glory."

While I walked down the line, I paused briefly beside each of the candidates, staring at their tools while I tried to imagine what they'd look like fully erect. But since there were only two black men in the lineup, my job was considerably easier, given the match in skin tones. When I stopped in front of the first black man who I remembered introducing himself as Linc, he tilted his head forward to peer at the photo in my hand, then he grinned.

"How hard can it be?" he said, turning his head to glance at the other African-American man three positions down the line. "There's only two of us."

"Well, you're kind of cheating," I said, glancing back and forth between the dick pic and his long, slightly curved dong. "The picture shows you shaved, but you're sporting a little stubble down there."

"Well, I didn't want to make it too easy for you," Linc smiled.

"I'll be back in a moment," I said. "Save that thought."

I took a quick glance at the TV screen, noticing that there was only two minutes remaining, then I scooted down the line toward the other African-American man, quickly comparing the dick pic to the real thing. Both men were circumcised and roughly the same size, but the second man's penis hung straight down, whereas my picture displayed a large curved erection, bending slightly to the side like a Japanese samurai sword. I jumped back into the now-chaotic swarm of shifting women, toward the first black man and smiled.

"You didn't disguise it that well," I said, grinning up at him. "You should have taken your picture from a different angle."

I turned his photo around, then slapped it against his hard pecs, watching his dick bounce excitedly once he realized I'd guessed him correctly.

"Okay ladies," Madison said, pointing toward the timer counting down on the TV screen. "You've got less than a minute remaining to make your decision. You better pin your pictures on your best guess, or you'll both miss your opportunity to participate in the next round."

Shae paused in front of the Hispanic newcomer named Diego, tilting her head up and down between the picture in her hands and the tan-colored organ dangling between his legs. Then she knelt down to take a closer look, blowing softly on his instrument, bobbing gently over his tightening balls as his blood coursed through his veins.

"Ahem," Madison said, shaking her head disapprovingly. "No touching and no teasing, Shae. You're cheating by helping him get an erection. You've got five seconds to make your decision."

"Fine," Shae said, standing up and slapping her photo against the handsome Latino's glistening chest. "I guess I'll just have to save the blowing part for later."

When the alarm finally sounded, the women stepped back from each of their chosen candidates, clapping and cheering loudly. None of them were sure they'd matched the penises correctly, but at this point it hardly mattered. For five glorious minutes, this had been the most fun any of them had had fully clothed.

**3**

———

"So, what happens now?" Shae said, peering at some of the men's penises beginning to rise and slowly hardening. "Do we get to play with the willies we correctly identified?"

"All in due time," Madison said, collecting the photos from each of the men's naked bodies and cross-referencing the letters on the back with a spreadsheet she held on a clipboard. She placed a check or an X beside each man's name, then she sat back down at the front of the group, smiling with a sly grin.

"We've got quite a few winners," she nodded. "But we'll have to wait until the results of the next contest to see who'll be moving on to the next stage."

There was a collective groan in the room, with both the men and the women disappointed they'd have to wait to do more than just look at their partners' sexy body parts. But I knew from previous experience that this was all part of Madison's plan to ramp up the sexual tension for the best part still to come.

"Now it's time to turn the tables and make

the ladies squirm for a change," she smiled. "This time it will be the women's turn to let it all hang out while the men inspect their private parts in a game I like to call Matching the Curtains and the Carpet."

"But you told us to shave ourselves clean," Emma protested. "What if we don't have any fur down there to compare the upper half with?"

"I guess that will make it all the more interesting then," Madison nodded. "We can't make it too easy for the men to match your pussies. What would be the fun in that?"

Marco suddenly shifted on the sofa, straightening out his tool in his tightening pants.

"Will the women be completely naked like we were?" he asked hopefully.

"Of course," Madison grinned. "I'm an equal opportunity hostess."

"And will it be timed like the other contest?" Brad said.

"Like I said," Maddy nodded. "In this game, men and women are treated exactly the same."

"Will there be another squishy prize for the winner?" Shae said, glancing in the direction of Diego's still naked body.

"Absolutely," Madison said. "Though this one might not be so squishy by the time you finish with it."

"Mmm," Shae purred. "Do I get to be on the other side of the lineup this time?"

"Yes," Maddy smiled. "Though something tells me your partner will have a little less trouble than the rest of the men matching your body parts."

Everybody chuckled nervously, then the women stripped down and sat on the edge of the fireplace hearth, parting their legs slowly. After everybody got in position, the men ogled their naked bodies, darting their eyes up and down the row, soaking up the spectacle. When they saw Shae's big prick flapping over her glistening pussy, their eyes bulged, hardly believing their luck seeing a true hermaphrodite for the first time in the flesh.

"Is everyone ready to get started?" Madison said, pointing her phone toward the TV, preparing to restart the timer.

"I think some of the men are a little more ready than others," Shae said, noticing a few of the men's cocks standing at full attention while they gaped at the lineup of naked women.

"Fortunately, this game doesn't require the same degree of restraint as the last one," Madison smiled. "Though the other rules still apply. You'll have to match the owner of the pussy in your picture only by looking at your partner."

"You better stand a few feet back then, Linc," I said to the handsome African-American, noticing his half-erect cock angling gently to the side while it levitated almost a full foot in front of his rippling abs.

"I'll try to demonstrate proper respect for your temple," he nodded, feeling a drop of precum forming on the crown of his cock.

"Alright then," Madison said, tapping her phone to start the timer. "Let the revelry begin."

The men wasted no time rushing up to the row of women, quickly moving opposite their suspected matches and examining their pictures while they carefully inspected the figures of their partners. I couldn't help chuckling when I saw a small crowd forming in front of Shae, knowing there could only be one person holding a picture of her unique genitalia.

I guess everyone's somewhere on the continuum after all, I thought to myself, remembering the old saying that every individual harbors some degree of physical attraction to both sexes.

While I watched the women sitting on the edge of the bench with their legs spread apart, I glanced at the shaved pussies of the two women sitting next to me. Each of them had a unique shape and texture to the contours of their vulva, with some having straight, symmetrical labia, while others had curved and flappy folds. Just like individual snowflakes, everyone had a unique shape and tone, and I seemed almost as fascinated as the men were appraising the lineup of glistening, pink flowers.

After a few minutes, Linc finally stopped in front of me, standing between my parted legs with his enormous, tanned poker pointing toward my left breast.

"Looks like I guessed you correct," I smiled, licking my lips. "That thing is even more impressive when it's angry."

"Sorry," he said, glancing down at his hard-on dangling a string of precum six inches below his flaring helmet. "It's kind of hard to remain relaxed when I'm staring at a bunch of naked women."

"Don't apologize on my behalf," I smiled, feeling the juices beginning to dribble out of my pussy and down the insides of my thighs. "I'm enjoying the show just as much as you are."

"I'm not sure about this one," he said, pulling his photo closer to my snatch as he squatted between my legs, comparing the two images. "Can you give me any hints?"

I leaned forward a few inches to peer at his photo, then I glanced up at him with a smile, recognizing the familiar picture. When he saw my pupils dilating in recognition, his penis flapped excitedly, emitting another long string of precum down onto the floor.

"You better be careful there, big fella," I grinned. "Somebody could slip and fall on that puddle you're leaving on the floor."

"Good," Lincoln said, meeting my gaze with a brilliant white smile. "I can use every advantage I can get to keep you all for myself."

**4**

---

After the previous two contests, all the group members were pretty worked up, not only because everyone was still naked and staring at each other's genitals, but also because they were already anticipating the next hookup. But I knew Madison had carefully planned everything to ramp up the sexual excitement to make the final connections all the more satisfying. While the men shifted uneasily, trying to conceal their throbbing hard-ons, Maddy peered around the room, grinning like a Cheshire Cat.

"I'm happy to see most of the guys are still aroused waiting for the next contest," she said. "Because those cocks are going to need to be rock-hard to make it to the end of this one."

"Are we going to do more than just look at each other's genitals this time?" Neil asked impatiently.

"As a matter of fact, yes," Maddy smiled. "This one will be a very tactile event, indeed."

She reached behind the sofa and carefully lifted a tall stack of interconnected wood blocks resting on a platter, placing it in the middle of the coffee table between the two sofas.

"In this game we'll call Joystick Jenga, you'll be putting your stiffie to good use trying to beat your fellow contestants."

"Ugh," Neil groaned. "I was kind of hoping we'd have a chance to connect with each other a little more...intimately."

"Well, in this event you will," Maddy grinned. "The winner will be sucked off by the loser."

"But it's only going to be played with men?" Neil said, furrowing his brow in disappointment.

"And your point?" Maddy said.

"What if some of us aren't gay?"

"We told you to park your inhibitions at the door," Madison nodded. "I warned you in the invitation that there'd be multiple-gender pairings. If you're going to play the game, you have to agree to play by the rules."

Brad suddenly shifted uneasily in his chair, peering at his wife with a lopsided frown.

"How will we decide who's the winner and who's the loser?" he said, worried about stretching the boundaries of their admittedly open marriage.

"It's pretty simple," Madison smiled. "The loser is the one who topples the tower."

"Then who'll be the winner if there's nine of us still standing after it topples?"

"That will be the one the loser chooses to perform fellatio on," Maddy said matter-of-factly.

"You mean we actually get to choose?" Ryan suddenly perked up, licking his lips as he swiveled his head among the group of bobbing dicks awaiting the start of the game.

"Of course," Maddy said. "That makes it all the more interesting."

"In that case, I'd hardly call the one who topples the tower the loser," the gay man grinned while gaping at Lincoln's huge, slightly curved dick.

"I told you we were going to stretch more than your imaginations in this game," Madison smiled. "I guess we're about to see just how fluid everyone's sexual persuasions really are. Are you guys ready to get started?"

Neil squirmed uncomfortably in his seat, crossing his legs to conceal his hidden organ.

"What if we're not hard yet?" he said.

"Well, you better get working on that pretty fast," Maddy smiled. "Because it will be a hell of a lot harder to push the blocks out of the stack with a soft penis."

While the men slowly crowded around the edge of the coffee table, Neil began rubbing his flaccid dick, trying to make it rise for the occasion. As I peered at the rest of the men, I found it interesting that virtually everybody else was already ramrod hard, their phalluses bouncing proudly over their bellies while little drops of precum began forming on their glistening crowns.

Fluid indeed, I smiled, knowing most of the men officially identified as being straight. Whether they were turned on by the idea of the women watching them strut their manhood or by the realization that one of them would soon to be sucked off, I couldn't be sure. Either way, all of the women leaned in closer on the edge of our chairs, eager to watch the action.

"Okay," Madison said, placing a spinning game dial on the table and flicking the pointer. After it stopped spinning, it pointed toward the handsome Latino, Diego. "It looks like you'll be going first, Diego. Then we'll proceed clockwise around the table until someone topples the stack."

Diego paused for a moment while he squinted at the tower, trying to plan out his strategy.

"So we simply poke out any random block using our penis only?" he said.

"Exactly," Madison nodded. "No touching allowed with any other body parts."

Linc suddenly cleared his throat, bending over to examine the size of the blocks more carefully.

"What if, um, our dicks are too large to fit through the holes?" he said.

"That's why I had this set specially constructed by our in-house carpenter, Brad," Maddy smiled. "I anticipated this eventuality, and with each block roughly twice the size of a regular set, I think even you'll have enough room to poke the bear, metaphorically speaking."

"Humpf," Linc huffed, shaking his head doubtfully.

"Okay, Diego," Madison said, nodding toward the group. "Let's get the party started. The ladies are just as impatient as the men to see who's going to win this game."

"Alright," Diego said, moving his flapping johnson closer to the stack of blocks. "Here goes nothing–"

"I'd hardly call that nothing," Shae chuckled at the handsome Latino she'd picked out of the lineup earlier. "I just hope I'll be the first one to suck that beautiful flute before anyone else has a chance to."

**5**

———————

Diego bent his knees slightly and flexed his buttocks, touching the tip of his dick against a block in the middle of the stack. As he gently prodded the loose dowel, it slowly began to poke out the opposite side, until it finally fell with a loud plop onto the glass surface of the table.

"Woo hoo!" the women cheered as Diego carefully withdrew his throbbing organ from the hole in the stack.

"Hold that thought, Diego," Shae teased. "Because I've got something a whole lot wetter and tighter for you to insert that thing into when you finish up there."

Diego glanced over at Shae, his face flushing in excitement at the thought of fucking the hot transgender girl.

"Don't get me more distracted than I already am," he chuckled. "This is hard enough without imagining screwing someone as pretty as you."

"Okay, Ryan," Madison nodded toward the man standing next to Diego. "You're up next."

"Oh, I'm up for it, alright," the gay man smiled, peering over at Diego's beautiful instrument. "With any luck, I'll have a chance to beat Shae to the punch having my way with that beautiful cock."

He placed one knee on the side of the coffee table, then he angled his hips forward, tapping the end of a block a few inches above the hole that Diego had left. As he prodded the block softly, feigning an exaggerated humping action, the other end of the brick edged out the other side until it teetered on an angle, hanging by a thread. Ryan withdrew his penis from the hole, then he leaned over, rubbing his ass against the side of Diego's thigh while he blew softly into the hole.

"Hmm," he said. "This reminds me of another crevasse I'd like to insert my dick into. It's too bad this one's made of wood, because my stiffie could use something a little tighter than this stack of bricks to get off."

"If you play your cards right," I chuckled, watching the brick topple out of the other side. "You'll have your choice of ready candidates soon enough."

"Speaking of," Madison said, turning toward the next man standing clockwise in the circle. "It's your turn to go next, Neil."

I glanced at Neil's organ and noticed it was now standing at full attention, bobbing excitedly over his shaved balls while he stared at the other men's upturned erections.

This was absolute genius, I thought to myself, making eye contact with Maddy. Gay, straight, or bi, there was no denying this game had a bit of something for everyone. The gay and bi guys got to indulge their fantasies of watching a bunch of turned-on dudes displaying their manhood in all their glory, while the straight men got to show off for the women. All while the women got to indulge their own fantasies of watching two hot guys hooking up at the end of the game. I had no idea what she had planned for the women in the next round, but I was already as wet as a four-stroke engine.

Neil paused for a moment while he studied the stack of bricks, planning his best strategy. While the two previous men had chosen to remove blocks from the center of the tower, he seemed more interested in examining the edge of the stack where the bricks could be wedged out more easily from the side than from the middle. After a few seconds, he pointed the tip of his dick toward one near the bottom of the stack, surmising that the weight of the blocks above would provide more stability to his prodding of the delicate tower.

As he gently poked the block with his purple glans, I noticed a drop of dew on the wooden piece from his slippery tip. I wasn't sure if he was getting excited by the sight of all the women intently watching him using his joystick to move the block, or if he was beginning to look forward to the possibility of being sucked off by one of the men looking on from the other sides of the table.

While the block see-sawed from side to side, the women ooed and awed loudly, adding to the drama of the scene. When it finally slipped out of the stack and the tower leaned to one side, teetering precariously on the edge of toppling, the women's eyes suddenly flared, eagerly anticipating the straight guy receiving his first gay blowjob. But after a few seconds, the tower stopped swaying, leaning over like some kind of twenty-first century modernist apartment block.

"Now it's beginning to get interesting," Madison smiled, glancing at the tower and the next man in the line, Lincoln.

"You're up next Linc," she said. "But you better be careful. I don't think the tower can withstand much more stress at this point. I hope you've studied engineering or architecture, because there's no telling where the weak point is now."

"Unfortunately not," Linc sighed. "And I'm pretty sure my finance degree isn't going to offer much help. Except insofar as the way compound interest increases the value of a future payout. Because my interest has definitely been growing with every game you've introduced, and I don't know how much longer I'll be able to hold out."

He peered down at the dripping string of precum hanging off the end of his cock and frowned.

"Although I suppose a little lubrication will only help reduce the friction in this instance..."

He glanced at the hole in the side of the stack where Ryan had removed the last piece, then he knelt down on the floor, pointing his long erection toward a center block lower on the stack. As he began to prod the piece slowly out the other side, the stack gently tilted from side to side while the women stared with wide eyes at his enormous organ. But after the piece edged halfway through the stack, Linc's curved erection began rubbing against the inside of the hole, causing the tower to sway even more precariously.

He paused when he realized his predicament, knowing that if he prodded any further, the combined friction of his thickly curved tool in the confined space would push the tower over before he had a chance to poke it out the other side.

"Can I change my target halfway through?" he said, peering over at Madison.

"I don't see why not," Maddy smiled. "We didn't mention anything about that in the rules. As long as you eventually remove one block from the stack without toppling it, you're still in contention."

"Okay," Linc said, glancing at the gap Ryan had left in the side of the tower with his previous turn. "It's time to start thinking like an engineer instead of a finance major."

He pulled his dripping tool out of the middle of the stack and pointed the glistening tip toward the block immediately adjacent Ryan's missing piece on the opposite side. But as he tried to push it off to the side as Ryan had, his slippery cum made it hard to gain traction against the block, and he paused once again, shaking his head in frustration.

"Mmm," Ryan interrupted, flaring his eyes at Lincoln's dripping dagger. "Why don't you save some of that for me? I'll be happy to lick you clean if you drop the tower. I'm looking forward to impaling my face on that weapon."

"I'm afraid I don't lean that way," Lincoln frowned, swiping the end of his dripping dick against some of the other blocks to dry the tip. Then he pressed the new block more firmly with his tool, slowly edging it from side to side until it toppled a few inches beside the base of the tower. The stack swayed for a few moments, then eventually righted itself with only two narrow blocks remaining on the lower row to hold the rest of the tower up.

"Hmm," Madison nodded, appraising Lincoln's handiwork. "That was pretty ingenious. But something tells me you've just made the job that much harder for the next contestant."

She peered over at Brad, who was studying the tower carefully, and smiled.

"Looks like you're up next, Brad. Do you think you can survive one extra round?"

Brad glanced at his wife Laura who was grinning at him with an enormous smile, and cocked his head.

"I'll give it my best shot, babe," he said. "But I'm in unfamiliar territory."

"Something tells me you're about to be in some other unfamiliar territory pretty soon," she grinned.

**6**

———

Brad paused for a moment, trying to figure out his best plan of attack, then he swiveled his hips toward the side of the tower, pointing his hard-on a few inches above the two holes left by Ryan and Linc.

"It looks like the side pieces are a little easier to slip out than the middle ones," he said, prodding the end of one block tentatively with his flapping erection.

"You better be careful, dear," Laura teased. "You don't want to knock it over with your bouncing dick before you have a chance to push the block out."

"That's the problem," Brad frowned. "It seems to have a mind of its own right now."

"Typical man," I chuckled. "Always thinking with his little head instead of the big one."

While the rest of the women laughed out loud, he tilted his head in my direction, sneering in mock amusement.

Then he slowly resumed tapping the block with his penis, trying to edge it out of its space. But with each tap, the tower began to wobble further and further, and by the third knock, it had begun to build an unstoppable momentum over the narrow support beneath it, and he could only watch helplessly as it toppled in a loud crash onto the surface of the coffee table.

"Ohhhh!" the women groaned, unhappy the game was over so fast. But their attention soon shifted when they realized the best part was about to come, when the married straight man would have to perform head on one of the remaining contestants.

"So what happens now?" Brad said, feigning ignorance.

"You'll have to perform fellatio on one of the men," Madison smiled.

Brad peered around the circle at the collection of throbbing penises standing proudly erect, shaking his head in dismay.

"I wouldn't know where to begin..." he said.

"Oh, come now," Madison grinned. "It's not so hard. It's just like sucking a popsicle."

"A very warm one, filled with cream," Brad frowned.

"Nobody said you had to swallow it," Maddy chuckled. "Though the least you can do is let your partner cum in your mouth. That's what every man has expected of us since the beginning of time, right ladies?"

"Damn right," Shae nodded. "What's good for the goose is good for the gander. And believe me, I should know."

Brad turned to his wife and shrugged his shoulders as if seeking for her permission to proceed.

"What do you say, dear?" he said. "Do you have anyone in particular you'd like to watch me giving head to?"

Laura glanced around the circle, pausing when she noticed Lincoln's long, dripping tool.

"As much as I'd love to watch you suck Lincoln's giant python, I'm not sure you'd be able to get your mouth around that thing. Why don't we see if we can find someone who's endowed with a size more similar to your own, so you can appreciate what it feels like for me to suck your dick..."

She darted her eyes around the circle, pausing when she noticed Diego's handsome, caramel-colored erection. Then she glanced up at the Latino's chiseled face and smiled.

"What do you say, Diego?" she said. "Are you up for a little boy-on-boy action?"

"It's been a while since I tried it in college," Diego smiled. "But if I remember correctly, it feels pretty much the same once I close my eyes."

"You heard the man," Laura grinned, turning toward her husband, then tilting her head, instructing him to get on his knees.

When Brad glanced at Diego, his dick flapped unconsciously, betraying his excitement at the idea of participating in his first homosexual encounter.

"How do you want me to do this exactly?" he said to Diego.

"It's pretty straight-forward," Diego said, smiling in the direction of Laura. "I suppose if I stand, your wife will be able to watch everything more easily."

Brad paused for a moment, temporarily taken aback by the Latino's provocation, then he glanced toward Laura, and she nodded with a big grin.

"It's okay dear," she said. "I'll be with you in mind and spirit. Maybe you'll pick up a few pointers that you can pass along to me. Everybody says men are better at giving head than women. It shouldn't be so bad."

Brad took a deep breath, then he kneeled down in front of Diego's bobbing organ, gripping it tentatively with the tips of his fingers and edging his mouth closer toward the flaring tip. When he opened his lips and encircled the glans, he hesitated for a moment, then he closed his eyes and lowered his head, engulfing Diego's circumcised crown in his mouth. As he began to bob his head over the tip of his cock, Diego moaned softly, titling his head down to watch the straight man blowing him uncomfortably.

"Don't just bounce on it like some kind of bobbing head," Laura chided, watching the pair intently. "You have to use your tongue to make it interesting. Imagine you're sucking on my clit while you roll your tongue over my nub to turn me on. Just under the edge, that's where you men like it best."

Brad paused for a moment, listening to his wife's instructions, then I noticed the side of his cheek moving as he began to swirl his tongue around Diego's corona, edging his head slightly lower.

"Nnngh," Diego moaned, grabbing hold of Brad's head and pushing his dick further into his mouth.

"Yeah, baby," Laura said, egging her husband on. "Just like that. Suck his tip like a lollipop. Suck it like you want to get to the gummy center."

"Mmm," Brad began to moan along with Diego, getting into the rhythm as he thrust his own hips forward, dry-humping the air.

"Do you like that, baby?" Laura said, lowering her hand toward her pussy while she separated her legs, watching the two men rocking their bodies together. "Would you like to be on the other end of one of those blowjobs some time?"

"Mmm," Brad nodded, dropping his hand onto the tip of his dick, becoming increasingly aroused by his first time touching a man intimately.

"Focus, sweetheart," Laura said. "This is about your partner, not you. Cup his balls with your hand and tease him underneath his sack. It feels three times as good when you stimulate his other erogenous zones when you suck his cock. There'll be plenty of time for you later."

Brad nodded his head, then he raised his right hand, cupping Diego's tightening balls while he sucked his corona more vigorously. When Diego tilted his hips upward, Brad's mouth slid further down his shaft, engulfing half of his organ, and he suddenly choked.

"It's okay, baby," Laura interjected, continuing to guide her husband. "Try to relax your throat so you don't gag. You breathe through an entirely different channel. Concentrate on breathing through your nose while you slowly take him deeper."

Brad slowed his sucking action as he concentrated on his breathing, then he slowly took more and more of Diego's organ into his mouth while the Latino pressed more firmly on the back of his head, encouraging him to go deeper. Within a few minutes, he'd impaled Diego's entire pole in his mouth with his lips flaring around the base of his balls while the Latino humped his face with increasing urgency.

"Fuck, yes," Diego hissed. "Suck my balls. Don't stop–that feels so good."

"Jesus, baby," Laura grunted, slipping three fingers into her sopping pussy. "You're a natural at this. We're going to have to incorporate this into our love life more often. I had no idea what we'd been missing all this time."

"It's always better when you can do it two ways," Shae nodded along with Laura as she sank two fingers into her dripping slit while jerking her hard-on with her other hand. "He's only beginning to scratch the surface of the possibilities."

"Mmm, yes," Laura said, turning her attention between Shae's erotic display and that of her husband moaning atop Diego's buried organ. "Tickle the area behind Diego's balls with your other hand. I can see that he's getting close. I want to watch him dump his load down your throat."

When Brad threaded his other hand behind Diego's balls and began stimulating the area between his testicles and his anus, Diego placed both of his palms behind Brad's head, pounding his dick harder against his face.

"Oh God," he grunted. "I can't hold it any longer. I'm going to come. Don't stop, here it comes..."

Suddenly, the Latino grunted loudly as he buried his dick deep into Brad's throat while gripping his hair tightly, emptying his seed down his partner's gullet while he bent over in heaving spasms. It seemed to take Diego almost a full minute to stop cumming as his buttocks flexed and his hips shook in delirious pleasure. When he finally stopped shaking, he withdrew his dripping organ from Brad's mouth, while his partner stared at his engorged organ with bulging eyes.

As I marveled at how quickly a straight man could be turned, I peered at the rest of the men still standing around the coffee table, noticing each of them flapping their hard dicks until they came together in a Bellagio-style fountain onto the glass table, over the pile of tumbled bricks.

How fast the castle crumbles, I thought, rubbing my pussy along with the rest of the women looking on in rapt attention, feeling my own orgasm rapidly approaching...

7

———

"Well," Madison said, surveying the sticky mess on the coffee table. "It looks like everybody enjoyed that game even more than I expected. Why don't we take a little break while I clean up and prepare for the next round? You'll find some refreshments in the kitchen, and the powder room is down the hall to the left."

"Should we get dressed while we wait?" Neil asked.

"You can if you want," Madison said. "But we're going to be alternating back and forth between boy games and girl games, and based on the last contest, I expect everyone will enjoy them more fully naked."

While everybody shuffled off to the kitchen to enjoy some hors d'oeuvres, Madison swept the sticky Jenga bricks into a bucket then wiped the coffee table down with Windex and some paper towels. When the group returned to the living room, they noticed a row of yoga mats lying on the floor and a raised curtain hanging over the fireplace with a series of cut-out holes spaced about a foot apart.

"What's all this?" Shae said, squinting at the strange setup.

"This time it's the ladies' turn to have some fun," Maddy smiled. "In this game I call Ping Pong Basketball, each of the women will be given five ping pong balls which they'll have to fling through the holes."

"When you say fling," Shae chuckled. "I'm assuming you don't mean with our hands?"

"What would be the fun in that?" Madison grinned. "The men had to play their game hands-free, so I think it's only fair the women do the same in this contest."

I glanced toward Madison, bulging my eyes.

"You want us to fire the ping pong balls through the holes with our pussies?" I said.

"Why not?" she said. "Strippers have been doing it for ages. Plus, it's good exercise for your Kegel muscles. It's a good way to tighten up your pussy and learn more control during sex."

"How will we choose the winner?" Laura said, walking up to inspect the setup more closely.

"Simple," Maddy said. "The winner will be the one who gets the most balls through the hole."

"And what's the prize this time?" Shae said.

"The winner will get her choice of which contestant she wants to go down on her."

"I'm assuming I get to play the girl part this time?" Shae smiled.

"Yes," Maddy nodded, peering down at her bifurcated genitals. "Although you'll have your choice of which role you wish to play if you happen to win the contest."

"Mmm, I like the sound of that," Shae grinned.

"Okay, ladies," Madison said. "Are you ready to do this?"

"How do you want us to prepare?" Laura said, still somewhat confused about the game rules.

"Each woman will lie down next to one another on a separate yoga mat, facing the curtain. There's a bucket behind each hole that will collect the balls you manage to toss through the panel."

"Will this game be timed, like the first two contests?" the cute straight girl, Lily, asked.

"No, just like with the men in Joystick Jenga, there's a bit of a learning curve involved. You can take all the time you need to finish the contest. Are you all ready to give it a try?"

"I guess..." Lily said, peering at the other women with a worried expression.

"Alright," Madison said, placing a cup with five ping pong balls beside each yoga mat. "Assume the position."

The men moved in closer to the mats to watch the action, then Marco suddenly peered up at Madison with a lopsided smile.

"Can we stand behind the curtain to watch it more closely?" he said. "Maybe it will be easier for them to fling the balls at our open mouths."

"I'm afraid that will be a little too distracting," Maddy chuckled. "But don't worry, you'll have your chance to get behind the curtain soon enough. This is an all-girl contest, so you'll just have to enjoy the show from the sidelines."

The women lay down face-up on the yoga mats then they spread their knees apart, peering at the adjacent holes in the curtain roughly five feet away.

"How do we do this exactly?" Laura said, lifting a ball out of her cup. "That looks like a long way to fling a ball using only my pussy."

"It's a little bit like childbirth," Maddy nodded. "You need to relax and contract some of the same muscles, just faster and with a lighter weight. After you insert the ball inside your slit, flex your abdominal muscles and exhale quickly while simultaneously trying to relax your pelvic floor muscles."

"Okay," Laura said, smiling in the direction of her husband. "Are you watching this, honey? Maybe we can use this technique to practice for our next baby."

"I'm game if you are," Brad laughed.

Laura slipped the ball into her opening, then she tilted her hips upward, exhaling rapidly. The ball spilled out of her slit, landing a foot in front of her hips, bouncing softly to the base of the curtain.

"Hmm," she said. "I see what you mean about a learning curve. It looks like this will take a bit of practice."

"That's why I gave each of you five balls," Maddy nodded. "Why don't you try it next, Lily?"

The cute blonde glanced at the other women lying next to her on the mats, then she shyly slipped a ball between her parted thighs and grunted heavily. The ball flung out of her pussy with a loud fart sound, bouncing off the curtain a few inches beside her targeted hole.

"Did you just fart?" Shae said, turning her head toward Lily.

"I'm not sure if it was a pussy-fart or a fart-fart," Lily giggled, turning a deep shade of crimson. "But it seemed to work. I almost got the ball through the hole. Now it's just a matter of perfecting my aim."

"You heard the woman, ladies," Madison nodded. "Saddle up and load your weapons. It's not as hard as it looks."

Each of the women proceeded to insert a ball into their pussies, then they grunted and exhaled as Madison instructed, sending a volley of white orbs toward the curtain. Some of them passed through the holes and some of them bounced back off the curtain onto the floor. With each volley of rounds, the room erupted in a cacophony of grunts and fart sounds, until the women dissolved in a jumble of hysterical laughter. By the time they finished, nobody knew who'd fired the most balls through the hole, but they hadn't had so much fun playing with their pussies since they were teenagers.

## 8

"Well, you guys enjoyed that even more than I expected," Madison said, rising off the sofa to count the balls in the buckets.

"Who knew pussies could be used for such novel entertainment?" Shae chuckled. "I might have to incorporate this into my cabaret act. I don't think I've made a room full of strangers laugh this hard in ages."

"It certainly was entertaining," Madison nodded, pulling back the curtain to count the number of balls that had landed in each of the buckets. As she began counting off the number of successful shots for each contestant, the group cheered and clapped at the results.

"Laura ended up with two," she said, pulling the balls out of the bucket one at a time. "Not too shabby for a first-time effort."

"Hear that, sweetie?" Laura said, peering over at Brad. "I only landed two balls with my pussy. Story of my life."

"Don't worry," Brad said, winking toward Diego. "I have a feeling we'll be introducing a few more into our love life soon enough."

Everybody laughed, and Madison resumed counting the balls in each bucket.

"And Lily," Madison continued, reaching into the bucket in front of Lily's mat. "You managed to get three balls successfully through the hoop."

"Woo-hoo!" Lilly clapped excitedly. "I guess all that pussy-farting pays off once in a while."

"Let's see how Jade did," Madison chuckled, reaching into the next bucket. "Also, three. Are you sure you guys haven't practiced this before?"

"Not unless you count the endless hours practicing with my Ben-Wa balls," I smiled.

Madison continued down the line, counting each woman's bucket collection until she reached Shae at the end of the row. When she reached into the pail, she lifted five balls cupped in her two hands.

"It looks like Shae had a perfect score," she smiled. "As the winner, you get to choose which of the women you'd like to share your reward with."

"Mmm," Shae purred, sitting up to inspect the lineup of sexy women sitting next to her on the mats. "There's a lot of worthy candidates, to be sure..."

Then she noticed Laura darting her eyes between Brad and herself, nodding excitedly at the prospect of having sex with her first transgender girl.

"But I think it's only fair that I give Laura a chance to return the favor from the last round. That is, if she's game for a little ladyboy action?"

"Oh, I'm game, alright," Laura grinned, shifting her hips over the wet spot rapidly forming on her mat. "But how do you want me to do this? Madison said the loser had to go down on the winner. I'm not sure which part you want me to play with, the boy part or the girl part?"

"Why not both?" Shae smiled, raising an eyebrow toward Madison. "You said you've never had sex with anyone other than her husband before today. Here's your chance to stretch your boundaries while putting some of those newfound skills your husband just demonstrated to good use."

"Works for me," Madison nodded. "Assuming that is, that Brad's on board with the idea."

"Fuck, yes," Brad grunted, his semi-flaccid dick already beginning to rise at the prospect of watching his wife go down on the sexy t-girl.

"Okay then," Madison said, motioning for Laura and Shae to move over to the leather sofa. "Why don't you two make yourselves more comfortable? I think it will be easier for you to service Shae while she's resting on the sofa."

"Yes," Shae smiled, strolling over to the couch and spreading her legs far apart as her erect dick flapped excitedly over her dripping pussy. "I believe it will."

Laura gawked for a moment at her bi-sexual genitalia, then knelt down in front of her, peering up at her thin waist and plump breasts. Even though Shae had a fully-functioning male penis, in all other respects she looked, sounded, and behaved like a voluptuous, sexy woman.

"Jesus," Laura murmured. "I hardly know where to start..."

"Why don't you start with the familiar part, then work your way down?" Shae smiled. "I don't see any timer, so you can take your time exploring my body. Maybe your husband can give you some tips along the way."

"Mmm," Laura smiled, grabbing hold of Shae's throbbing hard-on with two hands and beginning to stroke it up and down. "You're a little bigger than he is, so I might have to use both of my hands in this case."

"I think you're going to need more than two hands to manage all of that," Brad chuckled, darting his eyes between Shae's dripping pussy and her bobbing hard-on.

While Laura continued to stroke Shae's instrument as she moaned softly, the rest of the group inched closer, fascinated watching the true hermaphrodite display her glistening genitalia for the whole room to see. The men, in particular, seemed fascinated by the brazen display of the futa girl, stroking their own cocks unconsciously while they gaped at her like she was some kind of circus attraction.

"That feels good, Laura," Shae grunted, watching her phallus sliding in and out of Laura's tight fists. "But I'd love to feel your mouth, too. I could use a little extra lubrication to enjoy this fully."

"Mmm," Laura grinned, licking her lips. "I thought you'd never ask."

Without hesitating, Laura took Shae's big organ into her mouth, eagerly sucking and licking the head in the same way she'd instructed her husband earlier.

"Yes," Shae groaned, nodding her head approvingly. "It's not so different from your husband, is it?"

"This part, no," Laura said, raising her head for a moment to smile at Shae. "But the rest of you, that's a different story."

Shae paused as she glanced up at Diego, who was watching intently from the other side of the circle, cupping his balls with one hand while he stroked his dick with his other.

"It's kind of nice to have my lower parts stimulated at the same time," Shae said. "Like your husband did earlier with Diego. Touch me like you touch yourself when you're alone sometimes. I want to feel your fingers in my pussy."

Laura peered up at Shae with wide eyes, then she

lowered her head over her throbbing tool as she slipped two fingers into the front of her slit, fucking her softly while she circled her tongue over her crown.

"Yes," Shae groaned. "Just like that. Caress my G-spot while you suck my dick. That feels so good."

"Holy fuck," Brad hissed from a few meters away, watching his wife go down on the sexy ladyboy. "This is the hottest thing I've ever seen."

"Even more than watching porn?" Shae grinned, watching him fapping his dick rapidly.

"I've never seen anything like this on PornHub," he huffed, gaping his mouth open in excitement. "Nothing with someone as beautiful as you, having both male and female body parts."

"Well, if your wife continues to perform like this, you two are welcome to borrow me whenever you please. Because these parts can be used to satisfy either one or you, or even both of you at the same time."

Brad's eyes suddenly widened imagining the possibilities, then he spurted into his hand, unable to control himself. As he hunched over, shaking in pleasure, Shae chuckled, grabbing hold of Laura's head.

"I'm going to come soon too if you keep touching me like that," she said. "Do you want me to come in your mouth, or would you rather watch?"

Laura paused for a second, lifting her head temporarily off Shae's dripping organ.

"I'd be happy to have you come in my mouth," she said. "But something tells me the rest of the group would prefer a clear line of sight. Can I suck your pussy and stroke your dick instead?"

"Absolutely," Shae nodded. "But I have to warn you. I

squirt almost as hard out of my pussy when I come, as I do from my cock. You might want to prepare yourself."

"Oh, I'm prepared alright," Laura grinned. "I haven't had this much fun playing with a pussy since, well, the last exercise we just participated in."

"Yeah, well, I'm about to blow soon, so get ready to stand back."

"Mmm," Laura said, pressing her face hard against Shae's sopping pussy while she buried her tongue deep inside her slit, glancing up while she massaged Shae's bulging cock with her slippery hands.

"Yes, baby," Shae grunted, rocking her hips more rapidly on the sofa while she watched Laura eating her cunt. "Fuck me with your tongue. I'm gonna come any minute. Oh God, I'm going to come so hard. Fuckkkkk...."

Suddenly, she lifted her hips off the sofa and her big prick exploded in a shower of strings jetting up toward the ceiling while her pussy began spraying juices out from the side of Laura's face. When Laura realized her partner was coming from both orifices, she pulled her head back as the whole room peered on in fascination, watching her squirt and spray her juices in every direction.

It didn't take long for every man and half the women in the room to orgasm soon after, while they pounded their dicks and dripping pussies with their balled-up fists, unable to control their overflowing pleasure taking in the erotic spectacle.

## 9

"Well, that was a lot of fun," Madison smiled after everybody recovered from their orgasms. "I hope you boys have still got some fuel left in the tank, because our next game will need you to be hard and fast in a different way. Can I ask each of you to clean up the mess you made on the floor while I reset the stage? We wouldn't want any of you slipping during the active contest that follows."

While the rest of the group dutifully cleaned up the wet spots on the hardwood floor, Madison rearranged the curtain in front of the fireplace, then she disappeared into an adjacent room to collect the materials for the next game. When she returned, she carried another bucket with a collection of nerf baseball bats resting upside down.

"What are you going to have us do now?" the full-figured girl, Paige, chuckled. "Play a game of nude softball?"

"You'll be hitting some balls alright," Madison grinned, pulling one of the bats out of the pail with a dripping blue tip. "But not the kind you're imagining. In this erotic version of the popular carnival game Whack-a-Mole, you'll be trying to club a darting penis instead of a poking woodchuck."

"That sounds painful," Lincoln said, crossing his legs unconsciously.

"It's not as bad as it sounds," Madison laughed, squeezing the end of the soft bat with her fist. "These clubs are made out of foam, so it shouldn't hurt if you manage to get struck with one."

"What's the blue stuff on the end?" Laura said, peering at the dripping bat.

"It's non-toxic body paint, easy to wash off. We'll need some way of verifying when you make contact. Something tells me after I reveal the prize for the winner that the men will want to hide the truth."

"And what's that?" Linc said, glancing in my direction. "Another sexual favor from our choice of contestants?"

"Yes and no," Maddy said. "You'll receive a sexual favor, but this time you won't know who's performing it. The winner will stay behind the curtain while I choose who'll stimulate you from the other side."

"Oooo!" the ladies whistled, teasing the men about the surprise twist.

"So how are we going to do this exactly?" Diego said, peering toward the tall curtain with the row of waist-high cut-outs.

"Each man will stand one-at-a-time behind the curtain, randomly choosing which hole to thrust his penis through while one woman on the other side will try to strike it with her bat before he withdraws it back through the hole. You must poke your dick through one of the holes at least five times to qualify for the prize. The winner will be the one who completes the contest with an unsoiled crotch."

"Do we have to be hard for this contest?" Neil said.

"It'll certainly be more fun that way," Madison chuckled. "For the participants on both sides of the curtain."

Ryan suddenly shifted uneasily, peering at the group of women rubbing their hands together in anticipation.

"So, this is a boy-girl contest this time?" he said. "What if we don't swing that way?"

"Like Diego said earlier," Madison smiled. "You won't be able to tell who's sucking your dick on the other side if you can't see them. It'll feel pretty much the same way no matter who's doing it."

"I like the sound of this," Laura grinned, rubbing her hands together. "We get to take out our frustrations on our men's cocks, then watch them get sucked off by somebody else for their reward."

"That's one way of looking at it," Madison laughed. "But it's all in good fun. Kind of like cracking open a piñata to get to the prize inside."

"Except in this case, the prize will be nice and creamy," Laura smiled.

"Exactly," Madison nodded, turning toward the men. "Who'd like to go first?"

The guys peered at one another for a moment, unsure who wanted be the first contestant, then Laura reached into the pail, pulling out one of bats.

"It looks like my husband is a little more ready than the rest of the group, judging by the angle of his erection," she smiled. "Can I have the first crack at turning his balls blue?"

"I don't see why not," Madison said, glancing at Brad's bobbing erection. "You know the drill, Brad. Get behind the curtain and let's see if you can tease your wife in a different kind of way."

Brad paused as he grinned at Laura, then he ducked behind the curtain while Laura gripped her bat tightly with two hands, tensing it over her shoulder. After a few seconds, his cock darted through the hole on the left side of the curtain and Laura lurched to the side, swinging her bat at the prodding penis, missing it by inches before it disappeared back behind the panel.

"Oooo," the women hooted, laughing at the novelty of the game.

"That's pretty fast, sweetheart," Laura said to her husband from the other side of the curtain. "But it's not always good to be fast when using your penis. Let me paint that pretty dick with my brush and I promise to clean it off later with my tongue."

"Nice try, baby," Brad chuckled. "If I manage to evade your strikes, I've got a good chance at getting sucked off by somebody else. You already had your turn with one of the ladies, isn't it only fair that I get my turn now?"

"We'll have to see about that," Laura taunted. "Let's see who's the more adept one when it comes to swinging. Poke that pecker through another hole and let me have another swipe at it."

Brad hesitated for a moment then his dick suddenly poked out the other side of the curtain, before Laura had a chance to adjust her position.

"Ha, I'm on to you now," she smiled, moving closer to the center of the curtain and spreading her legs apart, preparing to strike again.

This time, Brad stuck his cock through the same hole, and Laura quickly slapped her bat down on it, splattering the tip with blue paint.

"Ouch!" Brad squealed from the behind the curtain, clutching his cock with two hands. "That hurt!"

"Oh, come on," Laura chided. "It can't be that bad. Why

don't you come out while I'll kiss it better? It's somebody else's turn to run the gauntlet now."

When he stepped out gingerly from behind the curtain, the women cheered loudly, and he slapped the side of Laura's ass with his stained dick, smearing her with the paint.

"Alright," Madison nodded, happy to see everyone getting into the swing of things. "Who'd like to go next?"

One by one, each of the men took a turn behind the curtain, darting their erect cocks through the holes, eventually getting smeared by their partner on the other side, emerging with only their dignity hurt. The last man to go up was Linc, and as he retreated behind the panel, Madison peered toward the lineup of women, raising an eyebrow to see who wanted to take her turn this time. I raised my hand and nodded my head excitedly, and Madison motioned for me to approach the curtain.

"Do I at least get to know who'll be batting for me on the other side?" Lincoln said, watching the shifting shadow through the narrow holes.

"No way," Madison smiled. "This is a blind contest for the men. You're just going to have to suck it up for the next few minutes."

"That's okay by me," Lincoln laughed. "As long as my partner is prepared to suck it up from the other side when we're finished."

"I suppose that'll be up to you," Madison grinned. "Depending on how deftly you can wield that sword of yours."

**10**

———

I smiled at Madison, then spread my legs apart on the floor, holding my bat tightly with two hands, preparing to strike the first object that poked through the curtain. Knowing Linc had the largest cock in the room, I expected to make short work of him, easily tagging his oversize organ before he had a chance to pull it back through the panel.

But he was far faster than I expected thrusting it in and out of the holes, and as he moved from side to side with the agility of a linebacker, I barely missed him each time. By the time he successfully pushed his cock through the fifth hole, the entire room erupted in applause at his athletic accomplishment.

"Damn," I huffed in frustration. "That was harder than I expected."

"It was hard alright," Madison grinned. "But something tells me it's getting even harder while he awaits his prize behind the curtain. Who wants to be the one to finish him off?"

The women peered at one another for a moment, each

of them eager to take a turn playing with Lincoln's huge, curved pole. I tilted my head and put on my best puppy-dog face, begging to be the one chosen after my initial contact with Linc in the first game.

"Shouldn't it be one of the ladies who tagged their partners earlier?" Paige said. "I mean, technically, Jade lost this contest with Linc. Shouldn't we be sharing the spoils with the rest of the women?"

I glanced at Paige dumbfounded for a moment, tilting my head and mouthing the word 'bitch'.

The rest of the women laughed then Madison peered toward at me, shaking her head.

"Sorry, Jade, but I'm afraid she has a point." She nodded her head, motioning for Paige to approach the curtain where Lincoln already had his flapping hard-on poking out of one of the holes, awaiting his prize.

"Mmm," Paige purred, kneeling in front of his undulating organ. "Can I use any part I choose to stimulate him?"

"I don't see why not," Madison smiled. "That is, if you're okay with the idea, Linc?"

"Absolutely," Lincoln grunted from the other side of the curtain. "I like these kinds of surprises."

"Well then, first..." Paige smiled, leaning over toward to his arcing organ. "I just want to touch this beautiful erection. I've never seen a penis as big as this one before."

She clamped her two hands around Lincoln's throbbing tool, her fingers only reaching halfway around his shaft, with two hand-widths still separating her fists.

"Are you sure you don't need a little extra help with that?" I said, feeling my juices beginning to drip down the insides of my thighs while I watched her stroking Linc's enormous pole.

"I think I've got the matter well in hand," Paige smiled,

noticing his glans emitting a drop of precum while she stroked him harder.

"What does it feel like?" Laura said, gaping at his magnificent tool with bulging eyes. "Why don't you share your experience with the rest of us so we can at least enjoy it vicariously?"

"It's warm," Paige nodded. "Very warm, like a fresh-baked loaf of French bread coming out of the oven. And throbbing as hard as a fire hose."

"Oh my God," Emma groaned. "What I'd do to have my hands or my mouth impaled over that dagger."

"Fuck that," Laura said. "I want that thing deep up inside my pussy. Though I'm not sure how far he could get it in. I can't imagine I'd be able to take more than half his length."

"I'd be happy to find a way," Shae chuckled. "I've never seen anything like that. And believe me, I've seen a lot of dicks in my day."

"You guys are getting me all worked up talking like that," Paige murmured from the other side of the room. "You're making me wet just thinking about it."

"What are you waiting for then?" I said. "The least you can do is give him a proper fucking since you denied the rest of us the opportunity."

"Don't mind if I do," Paige smiled, hesitating as she contemplated how she wanted to take him.

She peered at the lineup of women salivating while they gawked at Linc's pulsating organ and she slowly stood up, turning around with her back to the curtain. Then she reached between her legs to grasp the tip of his glistening rod, bending her knees slightly to press it slowly inside her spreading slit.

"Oh God," Emma grunted again, slipping her fingers inside her dripping pussy. "This is almost as good as having the real thing. Put on a show for us, Paige. I want to imagine it's me riding on top of that horse."

"Like this, you mean?" Paige grinned, swiveling her hips slowly like she was performing an erotic dance, sinking Lincoln's organ deeper inside her with each shift of her hips. He began to moan behind the curtain and she smiled, raising her hands to her huge tits, squeezing them tightly while she pumped his veiny cock with her plump ass.

Somehow the combination of her beautiful, rotund figure rocking overtop of his huge phallus simply added to the excitement of the spectacle. We could only imagine how Lincoln was reacting behind the curtain, but the sound of his increasing moans told us everything we needed to know. While Paige slowly worked his long pole deeper and deeper into her pink pussy, each of the women rubbed their clits furiously, imagining it was them fucking his thick spear instead of her.

"Holy fuck," one of the men hissed behind us, and I peered over my shoulder to see Neil gripping his hard-on tightly with two hands while he spread his mouth open, twitching in delirious pleasure. Before long, everybody else in the room began stimulating themselves while they watched the beautiful redhead pumping her hips up and down over Lincoln's hard piston, while he grunted ever louder behind the curtain.

"Fuck, yes," Laura panted, watching Paige lower her pussy all the way down over his thick balls. "Fuck that beanstalk. I want to watch him blow his load inside you."

Unghh," Paige moaned, her cheeks growing redder while she tightened the muscles in her face. "I'm almost there. Are you about ready to pop off, Linc?"

"Absolutely," Linc grunted. "Can I come inside you?"

"I'm on the pill, so no worries," Paige huffed, squeezing her tits harder.

"Fuck, yes," Linc groaned from behind the curtain. "This feels insane. I haven't had anyone who's been able to take my whole length before."

"Let it go, baby," Paige panted, her sex flush beginning to roll down over her bouncing tits. "I'm going to come with you."

"Yes," Linc grunted, shaking the curtain rapidly behind Paige's rocking body. "Here it comes. I can feel your pussy clamping down on me."

Suddenly, Paige thrust her two hands over the front of her slit while she jilled her clit furiously, gaping her mouth open in ecstasy. When her orgasm finally washed over her like a ton of bricks, she hunched over, heaving her body up and down while we watched Linc's thick organ pulsing strongly as he emptied his load inside her. But the sound of their moans was soon drowned out by the collective groan emanating from all around the room while everybody orgasmed in tandem with the sexy couple. As I convulsed over my dripping fingers deeply embedded in my pussy, I glanced over at Madison, noticing her hand thrust down the front of her jeans while a deep flush rolled over her cheeks.

I guess we're not the only ones enjoying this little county fair, I smiled to myself. She must have been wetting her pants anticipating how much fun this was going to be for every one of us even before we arrived.

**11**

―――――

"Whew!" Madison said after everyone recovered from their orgasms. "I don't know about you guys, but that was a lot more fun than any county fair I've ever been to!"

"I think you're on to something here," I nodded. "Maybe you should start your own public fair with your own set of games. Something tells me it would be sold out in hours."

"Hmm," Madison grinned. "I'm not sure it would be legal, with the current state of public indecency laws. But I have thought more than once about starting up my own sex club."

"Go for it," Laura said. "We'll be happy to spread the word. Your parties are the best ever!"

"Thanks," Maddy smiled. "But I've still got quite a few activities planned for this event. Maybe you guys can be my guinea pigs and tell me which ones are the most fun."

"Absolutely!" Emma said. "What's next on the agenda? Isn't it the ladies' turn this time?"

"Right you are, Emma," Maddy said. "But this time we're going to mix it up a little bit. What kind of a country fair would it be without a few rides?"

"What kind of rides?" Shae said, pinching her eyebrows. "It's not like you can fit a roller coaster in your living room."

"Perhaps not," Maddy smiled, flipping over a cover to reveal a miniature pommel horse sitting next to the fireplace. "But we can fit a few solo rides in here. In this next event I like to call Ride-em Cowgirl, we're going to test your stamina."

I peered at the familiar sex machine from a slumber party I hosted where I invited the manager of the local adult store to demonstrate her offerings.

"Is that a Sybian machine?" I said, widening my eyes.

"Indeed it is," Madison nodded. "Have you had some experience using one before?"

"Maybe once or twice," I grinned.

"Then I guess you'll have a bit of a leg up, in a manner of speaking, competing in this contest. Because the winner will be the one who can last the longest without coming."

"What's the prize this time?" Laura said, wrinkling her forehead. "If we come on the machine, won't it be a little anticlimactic for the winner to have sex with the loser?"

"Not if the winner gets to take it home with her afterwards to enjoy many more orgasms on her own," Madison smiled.

"What?" Paige said, suddenly flaring her eyes. "The winner gets to keep the machine?"

"For a little while," Maddy nodded. "At least until I open my own club, where I could use a little help setting up shop."

"How does it work, exactly?" Emma said, strolling closer to the machine to squint at the diamond-shaped plastic dildo propped up in the middle of the seat.

"It's pretty simple, really," Madison said, walking over to

demonstrate the device. "You simply sit on the dildo while I adjust the controls to increase the vibrations."

"So, it's really just some type of glorified vibrator?" Emma said, rubbing her hand over the strangely shaped dildo.

"Well, yes," Maddy smiled. "But I think you'll find it's like nothing you've ever tried before. In addition to the vibration embedded in the unusually shaped dildo, the seat of the machine also vibrates. It's quite a stimulating experience, if I do say so myself."

"Now I see why you call it Ride-em Cowgirl," Shae nodded. "It kind of looks like riding a horse."

"Yes," Madison grinned. "A very sexy and hung horse."

"So, who'd like to be the first to give it a try?" Madison said, glancing around the group of women. "What about you, Emma? You seem particularly fascinated with the shape of the device."

"Okay," the pretty blonde said. "But why is the dildo shaped like a diamond?"

"You'll just have to see for yourself," Maddy smiled. "You know what they say–a diamond is a girl's best friend."

"We'll have to see about that," Emma nodded, straddling the saddle and turning her head toward Madison. "Is there a proper way to sit on it?"

"You can position yourself in either direction," Madison said. "But I think if you face the front of the room, the rest of the group will be able to enjoy it almost as much as you."

"Okay," Emma said, squatting down over the dildo and flaring her eyes when the knob slipped inside her pussy.

"It's a little smaller than some of the other cocks I've

sampled," she smiled, twisting her hips seductively on the seat.

"Maybe so," Maddy said, lifting the electronic controller attached to the device and beginning to turn the dial. "But can the other cocks do this?"

She twisted the dial slowly, and the machine began to hum with the plastic plate holding the dildo to the frame flapping softly in front of her slit.

"Oh!" Emma squeaked, raising her eyebrows. "That's a little different..."

"Different good?" Madison grinned.

"Yes," Emma grunted, rolling her hips gently over the apparatus. "Very good."

"It gets even better," Madison smiled, twisting the dial a little further clockwise.

"Oh my God," Emma groaned, placing the palms of her hands on the front of the machine to support her quivering body. "That feels incredible."

"Better than your usual vibrators?"

"Yes," Emma purred. "There's something about sitting on top of it and being able to ride it like a–"

"Horse?" Madison grinned.

"Something like that," Emma grunted.

"Well hold onto your britches, because this horse is about to start galloping..."

Madison twisted the dial all the way to the maximum setting, and Emma suddenly threw her head back, spreading her legs wide apart while her tits bounced excitedly on her chest.

"Holy shit," she panted, gaping her mouth open in pleasure while the whole group watched her shaking atop the vibrating device. "This is crazy. I can't hold it much longer..."

"Just let it go, baby," Madison said, smiling while she

watched the flush on Emma's chest spreading up her neck toward her twisted face.

"Ngah!" Emma suddenly cried out, slumping over the front of the machine as her whole body convulsed in a powerful orgasm.

## 12

"Not too bad," Madison said, turning down the vibration as Emma began to stop shaking. Then she peered at her stopwatch and nodded. "Ninety seconds. That's longer than I lasted when I first tried the machine."

"Maybe I had a little stage fright holding me back," Emma smiled, lifting herself gingerly off the dripping dildo. "It was a bit more difficult trying to concentrate while everybody was watching me."

"Some people get off even faster on that," Maddy nodded. "Who'd like to try it next? What about you, Laura? This is your chance to try out a different kind of cock. Though this one mightn't be quite as warm and juicy as Shae's."

"True," Laura said, smiling toward the sexy transgender girl. "But she denied me the chance to sit on her pretty cock earlier. I've been wanting a hard dick up my cunny ever since the first Shower versus Grower game."

"Give me a moment to clean the machine and get it

ready for you," Madison said, wiping off the glistening dildo and the surrounding area with a moist cloth.

"Alright," she said when she finished. "Your chariot awaits."

"Don't get too comfortable on that thing, sweetheart" Brad teased as she straddled the apparatus and slowly lowered herself over the upturned dildo. "I'm not sure I'll be able to compete with an automated dick machine."

"Maybe not in terms of recovery time," Laura grinned as she inserted the hard plug into her hole. "But you're certainly a lot prettier than this machine."

"All set to begin?" Madison said, placing the controller in one hand and her stopwatch in the other.

"As ready as I'll ever be," Laura grinned, winking toward her husband.

Madison turned the dial partway to the way to the right, and when the machine started humming, Laura's eyes flew open, surprised at the intensity of the device.

"Okay," she nodded. "That's definitely not like any other dildo I've tried before."

"How does it feel different?" Brad said, his dick already starting to rise while he watched his wife ride the vibrating machine.

"It's hard to describe," Laura grunted. "It's more of a full-body experience, like when I'm riding on top of you. Just more–"

"Intense?" Brad said, wrinkling his forehead.

"Well, your dick doesn't exactly vibrate when you're inside me," Laura chuckled, rolling her hips over the undulating platform.

"Or change speed automatically," Madison smiled, twisting the dial further to the right.

"Unghh," Laura panted, placing her hands overtop of her thighs to support herself while she rocked on the shaking machine. "This feels so good. Maybe you should try it sometime, honey. Gay guys say the anus has as many nerve endings as a woman's pussy."

"Well, I'm not gay," Brad grinned, watching his wife becoming more turned on with each passing moment. "But I can think of some other ways we might enjoy that machine together."

"I'd like that," Laura grunted, locking eyes with him while she squeezed her shaking tits. "You could press your dick against me while you hold me, and we could enjoy the vibrations together."

"Yes, baby," Brad said, stroking his cock while he imagined the two of them riding the machine together. "But I don't know how long I'd be able to last with you looking so hot on that thing."

"I'm going to come soon," Laura hissed. "Watch me while I come for you. Oh baby..."

As she tilted her head back in escalating ecstasy, Madison turned the wheel to the maximum setting, and suddenly Laura's body began jerking while her thighs slapped against the side of the frame. Both she and Brad gaped their mouths open in pleasure while the rest of the group looked on in rapt attention, feeling their own erogenous zones pulsing in unison with the happy couple.

When Laura finally stopped coming, Madison turned off the machine and peered at her watch.

"Two minutes, ten seconds," she nodded, making a notation on the clipboard beside her. "A little better than Emma, but I think you had a little help from your husband."

∼

AFTER LAURA GOT off the machine and Madison wiped it down, each of the women took a turn on the device, lasting anywhere from one to three minutes before climaxing in uncontrollable pleasure. Nobody seemed prepared for the unusual combination of the vibrating platform shaking under their ass and the pulsating dildo purring inside their pussies. With Madison expertly controlling the progression in pleasure, none of them had a chance holding out for more than a few minutes.

When it finally became my turn to ride the machine, I hesitated overtop of the diamond-shaped dildo, trying to slow my pulse and my breathing. When I lowered my pussy over the plug, I closed my eyes, trying to shut out the distractions from the rest of the room, knowing that watching my friends playing with themselves while I squirmed over the hotseat would only add to my excitement.

While Madison slowly ramped up the speed of the undulating dildo, I tried to think about work and other boring topics, but the sensation of the vibrating horse and the shaking dildo eventually turned my attention to the escalating pleasure emanating from my midsection. As much as I tried to resist the rising crescendo, after a few minutes, my body succumbed to the pressure, unconsciously rocking in symbiosis with the machine.

As my orgasm slowly began to spread across my pelvis, I contorted my face, trying to hold it off as long as I could. But when Madison turned the dial all the way to the max, I let out a high-pitched squeal, pulling my thighs hard against the side of the machine and spraying out my juices in every direction while I shook uncontrollably in undeniable pleasure. When I finally stopped shaking, Madison turned off the machine and peered at her watch with a lopsided grin.

"Wow," she said. "Maybe I should try closing my eyes more often when I have sex. You managed to hold out for an impressive four and a half minutes during that ride. That puts you in first place, with only one contestant to go."

## 13

Madison glanced in Shae's direction and the t-girl peered back at her with a surprised expression.

"You mean I get to participate with the women again?" she said excitedly.

"Of course," Maddy smiled. "You've got an innie like the rest of us, don't you?"

"Well, yes," Shae grinned. "I've got both an innie and an outtie. I seem to have an unfair advantage being able to play on both sides of the table."

"Well, it looks like the rest of the group doesn't seem to mind," Madison said, noticing everyone inching closer to the machine to watch the sexy transgender girl ride the device. "It seems that they're just as excited as I am to see if you'll experience twice the pleasure with twice the equipment."

"We'll have to see about that," Shae nodded. "I normally have multiple partners to stimulate me when I have sex. This time it'll be only my girl part that has a chance to get stimulated."

"I suppose that answers the question about which part of your introduction was a truth versus a lie," Madison chuckled. "Something tells me you'll have no shortage of willing partners after we finish this first phase of the party."

"You mean there's more to come after this?" Shae said, widening her eyes in surprise.

"We're just getting started," Madison nodded. "We're only about a third of the way through the planned events. I hope you guys will still be able to get it up after getting your rocks off so many times. Because the remaining events won't work very well with a soft dick."

Shae chuckled while she glanced down at her bobbing hard-on, already beginning to get excited about the prospect of riding the sex machine in front of the rest of the group.

"Oh, I'm up for it alright," she smiled. "Like Jade said earlier, this thing has a mind of its own."

"Have a seat then," Madison said, motioning for Shae to sit on the device. "I think her time will be pretty hard to beat."

"She always sets the bar high," Shae nodded, peering over in my direction. "Ever since we compared cucumbers at the grocery store, I knew she had a unique talent."

While Shae lowered her pussy over the plastic dildo, everyone crept in a little closer, watching her big dick pointing up over the base of the machine like the tall horn of a saddle. Everybody knew this was going to be a special show, and the men were already stroking their dicks, excited to watch the sideshow distraction.

"Are you ready?" Madison said, holding the controller in her hand.

"Not as ready as everybody else seems to be," Shae chuckled, peering at the circle of men gawking at her with wide eyes.

"Here goes nothing, then," Madison said, twisting the knob slowly.

"Uhnn," Shae groaned as she felt the vibrating dildo shaking inside her pussy. "That feels exquisite. I've never had a vibrator stimulating my pussy and the base of my cock at the same time."

"Take your time and enjoy it, sweetie," Madison purred, twisting the dial a little slower than with the others. "I know the rest of us surely will."

Shae glanced down, noticing her cock emitting a drop of precum, and smiled.

"Do you mind if I touch myself while you stimulate me?" she said. "I'd kind of like to jerk off with the rest of the guys to enjoy this experience fully."

"No problem on my end," Madison grinned. "But I don't know how much that will help you hold out longer to win the game."

"I don't care about winning," Shae said, gripping her hard-on tightly with two hands. "I've already hit the jackpot watching this group of hot men and women staring at me while I get off."

"Suit yourself, babe," Madison said, turning the dial further to the right.

"Mmmh," Shae grunted, rocking her prick in and out of her hands while she squirmed her hips over the seat of the machine. "Bring it on. Give me everything you've got."

Madison grinned while she watched the rest of the group rubbing their crotches as they gazed at the sexy t-girl stroking her dripping dick. She knew Shae wouldn't be able to last much longer and while she watched her squirming over the machine, she lost track of time, rocking her hips in synchronicity with Shae. She didn't even have to touch herself, feeling her pleasure rising in lockstep, lost in the passion of the moment.

When she noticed Shae's mouth beginning to gape open on the brink of climax, she began to feel her own pleasure approaching the tipping point. She turned the speed dial all the way to the right, and they both climaxed together, shaking powerfully in their respective chairs. While Shae shuddered atop the machine, jetting long arcs of spunk toward the gallery, the entire room groaned in simultaneous pleasure taking in the erotic scene.

After Madison indicated that her time was second to my own, I hard cared. All I could think about was how much I wanted to use the machine in tandem with Shae, sitting atop her pretty cock while we both came together over the shaking horse.

*READY FOR MORE EROTIC chills and thrills? Read the next volume in Jade's Erotic Adventures: Carny Games 2. Buy direct and save at victoriarusherotica. Or download from your favorite online bookstore here: retailer links.*

*The carnival games require a whole different kind of skill...*

# ALSO BY VICTORIA RUSH

## Adult Fairytales:

The Enchanted Forest: An Erotic Fairytale

The Land of Giants: An Erotic Fairytale

The Dragon's Lair: An Erotic Fairytale

Witch's Brew: An Erotic Fairytale

The Mage's Spell: An Erotic Fairytale

The Mermaid Lagoon: An Erotic Fairytale

The Coven: An Erotic Fairytale

Rapunzel: An Erotic Fairytale

The Seven Dwarfs: An Erotic Fairytale

The Land of Mutants: An Erotic Fairytale

The Erotic Temple: A Sexy Fairytale (Coming Soon)

**Erotica Themed Bundles:**

Voyeur: Lesbian Erotica Bundle

Public Affairs: A Lesbian Anthology

Futa Fantasies: The Ladyboy Collection

Threesomes: The Lesbian Collection

Threesomes - Volume 2: The Lesbian Collection

First Time: A Lesbian Anthology

Hedonism: An Erotic Anthology

Switch Hitters: Bisexual Erotica

Taboo Erotica: The Lesbian Series

BDSM: The Lesbian Collection

Party Games: The Erotic Collection

Party Games 2: The Erotic Collection

All Girl 1: Lesbian Erotica Bundle

All Girl 2: Lesbian Erotica Bundle

All Girl 3: Lesbian Erotica Bundle

All Girl 4: Lesbian Erotica Bundle

**Erotic Fairytale Bundles:**

Clover's Fantasy Adventures: Books 1 - 5

Clover's Fantasy Adventures: Books 6 - 10

**Erotic Fantasy:**

Pirate's Bounty: A Time Travel Adventure

Wild West: A Time Travel Adventure

Private Riley: A Time Travel Adventure

Cleopatra's Secret: A Time Travel Adventure

Bounty Hunter 2125: A Time Travel Adventure

Ninja Assassin: A Time Travel Adventure

The 300: A Time Travel Adventure

Arabian Nights: An Erotic Fairytale (coming soon...)

**Steamy Time Travel Bundles:**

Riley's Time Travel Adventures: Books 1 - 5

**Lesbian Erotica:**

The Dinner Party: Lesbian Voyeur Erotica

The Darkroom: Bisexual Voyeur Erotica

Naked Yoga: Lesbian Transgender Erotica

Nude Cruise: Bisexual Voyeur Erotica

Rush Hour: Taboo Public Sex

The Girl Next Door: First Time Lesbian Erotic Romance

Girls' Camp: Lesbian Group Sex

Wet Dream: Ladyboy Fantasy Erotica

The Convent: Taboo Sex with a Nun

Sex Robot: A Dream Sex Machine

The Personal Trainer: Getting Pumped at the Gym

The Dominatrix: BDSM Lesbian Domination

Webcam Chat: Lesbian Online Sex

Paint Me: A Kinky Bodypainting Workshop

The Toy Party: Girls Sharing Sex Toys

The Costume Party: Strapping One On

Swedish Sauna: Lesbian Group Sex

The Therapist: Taboo Lesbian Erotica

Elevator Shaft: Bisexual Threesomes Erotica

Ladyboy: Lesbian Transgender Erotica

Peep Show: Lesbian Voyeur Erotica

The Dare: Public Sex Erotica

Maid Service: Lesbian Threesomes Erotica

The Hitchhiker: First Time Lesbian Erotica

The Housesitter: Spycam Lesbian Erotica

The Spa: Lesbian Group Orgy

Parlor Games: Blindfold Sex Party

The Exchange Student: First Time Lesbian Erotica

The Hostel: Bisexual Group Erotica

The Harem: Lesbian Erotic Romance

The Orient Express: Lesbian Voyeur Erotica

The First Lady: A Forbidden Lesbian Erotic Romance

The Slave: Lesbian BDSM Erotica

The Masseuse: Lesbian Sensuous Erotica

Too Close for Comfort: Lesbian Forbidden Erotica

Naked Twister: A Wild Party Game

Lexi: The Sex App ( Lesbian Fantasy Erotica )

Call Girl: Lesbian Bisexual Threesomes Erotica

Circle Jill: Lesbian Masturbation Workshop

The Viewing Room: Masturbation Voyeur Erotica

Spin the Bottle: A Kinky Party Game

The Hair Salon: Lesbian Voyeur Erotica

Tribadism 1: Girls Only Sex Workshop

Tribadism 2: The Art of Scissoring

Tribadism 3: Threeway Hookups

The Kiss: A Game of Oral Sex

Pledge Week: Sorority Sisters

Carny Games 1: A Wild Sex Party

Carny Games 2: A Kinky Sex Party

Carny Games 3: An Erotic Sex Party

Dreamscape: An Artificial Reality Game

Glory Hole: Guess Who's On the Other Side

Joy Ride: A Late Night Erotic Bus Trip

The Blind Girl: An Erotic Romance(Coming Soon)

**Lesbian Erotica Bundles:**

Jade's Erotic Adventures: Books 1 - 5

Jade's Erotic Adventures: Books 6 - 10

Jade's Erotic Adventures: Books 11 - 15

Jade's Erotic Adventures: Books 16 - 20

Jade's Erotic Adventures: Books 21 - 25

Jade's Erotic Adventures: Books 26 - 30

Jade's Erotic Adventures: Books 31 - 35

Jade's Erotic Adventures: Books 36 - 40

Jade's Erotic Adventures: Books 41 - 45

Jade's Erotic Adventures: Books 46 - 50

Fifty Shades of Jade: Superbundle

**Standalone Stories:**

The Polynesian Girl: A Lesbian EroticRomance

# FOLLOW VICTORIA RUSH:

*Want to keep informed of my latest erotic book releases? Sign up for my newsletter and receive a FREE bonus book:*

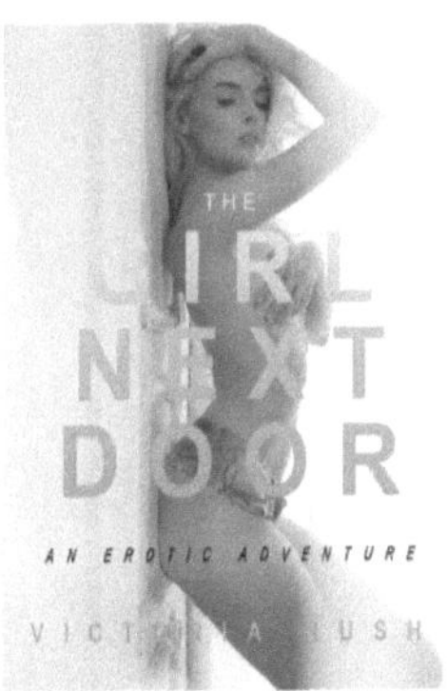

*Spying on the neighbors just got a lot more interesting...*